Kenji Miyazawa Picture Book Series-1

The Shining Feet

Original text by Kenji Miyazawa
Translated by Sarah M. Strong
Pictures by Miyuki Hasekura

Sarah M. Strong
Feb. 26, 1997

International Foundation for the Promotion of Languages and Culture
(IFLC)

The Shining Feet

Kenji Miyazawa Picture Book Series -1

First Published 1997

Special thanks to Miyazawa Kenji Museum and
Miyazawa Kenji Iihatobu Museum
Original Text: Kenji Miyazawa
Translation: © Sarah M. Strong 1997
Book Design: Seiichi Suzuki
Illustration: © Miyuki Hasekura 1997
Proofreading: Earnest Marvin Smith
Published by International Foundation for the Promotion of Languages and Culture (IFLC),
Sunmark Bldg., 1-32-13, Takadanobaba, Shinjuku-ku, Tokyo, 169, Japan
TEL: 81-3-5273-6660 FAX: 81-3-5273-6661
Publisher: Keiichi Kajikawa
Circulated by Sunmark Inc., Sunmark Bldg., 1-32-13, Takadanobaba, Shinjuku-ku, Tokyo, 169, Japan

ISBN4-7631-2311-4 C8390

Contents

One: The Mountain Hut

Outside the birds were making so much noise that Ichiro woke up.

It was already broad daylight.

From the corner of the hut, three rays of bluish sunlight streamed at an angle directly over the heads of Ichiro and his little brother, lighting up the hatchet and pair of straw leggings that hung on the reed wall opposite.

In the center of the earthen floor a brushwood fire was burning brightly. It was the smoke from the fire that made the shafts of sunlight appear blue. The smoke twisted and curled into all sorts of shapes as it drifted upward, passing through the bars of light.

"Sun's up already," Ichiro said to himself as he rolled over to face his younger brother, Narao. Narao's face was as red as an apple. He was still sleeping peacefully, his mouth slightly open. Catching a glimpse of whiteness within, Ichiro abruptly reached out and snapped his finger against Narao's teeth.

Narao's face grimaced a little, but his eyes remained shut and he continued to sleep, his breath coming in a soft whistle.

"Wake up, Narao. It's morning. Wake up," said Ichiro as he rocked Narao's head gently back and forth.

Narao frowned and muttered something, clearly reluctant to wake up, but he eventually opened his eyes a crack.

Then his face took on a surprised look and he murmured, "Hey, we're in the mountains. I forgot."

"The fire went out sometime during the night. Did you notice?" Ichiro asked.

"Uh-uh."

"It was real cold, but it seems Dad got up and started it going again."

Narao did not say anything to this. He had a distant look on his face as though he were thinking of something else.

"Dad's outside working. Let's get up."

"Okay."

The two boys got up from the single small quilt, in which they had slept bundled together, and went over to the fire. Narao rubbed his eyes as though the smoke were bothering him while Ichiro gazed steadily at the flames.

Outside, the mountain creek flowed with a roar and birds called shrilly.

Suddenly, brilliant golden sunlight streamed toward Ichiro's feet.

He looked up to see the door swing open and his father enter the room. His father appeared inky black against the view of snowy mountain so brilliantly white it almost hurt Ichiro's eyes to look.

"Ah, so you're up. Were you cold last night?"

"No, Dad."

"The fire kept going out. I got up twice to start it up again. Better go wash up now. Breakfast is ready. Okay, Narao?"

"Okay."

"Which do you like best, here in the mountains, or home?"

"I like it here in the mountains best, but it means we can't go to school."

Their father chuckled as he raised the cooking pot a little. Ichiro stood up and went outside, followed by Narao.

How beautiful it was. The sky glistened with a glossy blue light that was so bright it made their eyes tingle. When they looked up at the sun, it was like a huge gemstone in the sky giving off shining specks of green and orange and all sorts of colors. Dazzled, they closed their eyes and in the blueblack darkness they seemed to see the sun shining bluely. When they opened their eyes once again they found that lots of shadow images of the sun, gold and deep purple and other colors, were spinning and trembling in the same blue sky they had seen before.

Ichiro cupped his hands to catch the flow from the water pipe. A long icicle extended in a thick column from the lip of the pipe. The water shone transparent in the sun and gave off a steamy vapor that made it look warm although in fact it was very cold. Ichiro quickly rinsed out his mouth and then washed his face.

His hands were so cold that he stretched them out towards the sun, but when the sun failed to warm them he pressed them against the skin of his neck instead.

Narao was trying to imitate everything that Ichiro did, but after a while his hands got so cold that he quit. Narao's hands were all red and swollen from frostbite.

"Are your hands cold?" asked Ichiro as he hurried over to Narao and wrapped his own hands around Narao's damp, little red ones in order to warm them.

The two boys went back into the hut.

Their father was gazing into the fire, lost in thought. The lid of the pot made a soft, steady rattle. The two boys sat down. The sun was now well up, and the slant of the bars of bluish sunlight was steeper. The snow on the mountain stood out boldly against the blue sky. Looking at it somehow made one's heart seem to fly off into the distance.

Suddenly something blurry and white like smoke or mist appeared on the summit.

A moment passed and then a high, shrill voice that was like a flute reached their ears.

At the sound of the voice, Narao tensed his lower lip and a look of distress came over his face. For some reason, after a moment or two, he began quietly to sob. Ichiro looked at him in surprise.

"What's the matter, Narao? Do you want to go home? What's the matter?" the father asked. But Narao just put his two hands to his face and, instead of answering, cried louder.

"What's bothering you, Narao? Does your stomach hurt?" Ichiro asked, but Narao just continued to cry.

The father stood up and felt Narao's forehead, then he cradled Narao's head firmly in his hands.

Narao's crying gradually subsided until finally all that was left were a few broken sobs.

"Why are you crying? I wonder if it's because you want to go home?"

"Uh-uh," Narao, still making little shuddering sobs, shook his head.

"Does it hurt somewhere?"

"Uh-uh."

"Then why are you crying? A man doesn't cry, right?"

"I'm scared," Narao, still sobbing, managed finally to reply.

"Why are you scared? I'm here and your brother's here and it's a bright, sunny morning and so there's absolutely nothing to be scared of, right?"

"Yeah, but I'm scared."

"Why are you scared?"

"'Cause of what Matasaburo the Wind Boy said."

"What did he say? Matasaburo the Wind Boy isn't scary. What did he say?"

"He said my father would dress me in new clothes."

Narao started crying again. For some reason Ichiro felt a cold shiver go up his spine, but his father just laughed.

"Ha, ha! Matasaburo the Wind Boy told you something good. Come April I'm going to buy you some new clothes. There's nothing at all to cry about. You can stop that crying now."

Ichiro peered into Narao's face as he sat beside him. "Don't cry, Narao," he said, trying to comfort his little brother.

"He said more." Narao's eyes were red from rubbing.

"What did he say?"

"He said that my mother would put me in a warm bath and wash me."

"Ha, ha! Now that was a lie. Why, you're big now and take your bath all by yourself. That Wind Boy is

quite a liar. Now, don't you cry."

Their father's face looked somewhat pale and he seemed to be forcing himself to laugh. For some reason, Ichiro's chest felt tight and he couldn't bring himself to smile. Narao still did not stop crying.

"We're going to eat now, so no more crying."

Rubbing his eyes that now looked strange, all red and small, Narao looked at Ichiro and murmured, "Then he said that everyone will go together to see me off."

"Everyone will go together to see you off? Why that means when you get big and important and have to go somewhere, everyone will see you off together. All the things he said were good things. So don't cry. When spring comes, I'm going to take you to see the festival in Morioka, so there's no need to cry, right?"

Ichiro's face was very pale and he gazed silently at the fire that was lit by the sunlight.

Finally he said to Narao, "There's no reason to be scared of someone like that Wind Boy Matasaburo. He's always saying all sorts of things just to fool people."

Narao's crying gradually quieted to occasional shuddering sobs. Perhaps because he had been crying and rubbing his eyes in the smoke, his face all around his eyes had turned black and he looked like a little raccoon.

His father laughed, but somehow it sounded more like a sob.

"Hey, you need to wash that face again," he said as he stood up.

Two: The Pass

By afternoon the roar of the mountain stream had changed. It sounded somehow warmer and also more peaceful. The boys' father stood at the door of the hut talking with a man who had come up to the mountains with his horse in order to buy the charcoal the father made. The men talked for a long while, then the charcoal dealer started to load the bags of charcoal onto the horse. The two boys went to the doorway and watched.

The horse chomped hungrily at its feed. Its brown mane was bushy and ungroomed. The horse's eyes were very large and all sorts of strange mechanical devices seemed to be visible inside them, so that it looked quite pitiful.

The father turned to Ichiro and Narao, "Now you two boys are to follow this man and go back home. He can take you 'cause he's going all the way to Narabana. Next Saturday, if the weather's good, I'll come and get you, okay?"

Since the following day was Monday, the boys both needed to return home in order to go to school.

"So then, we'll be on our way," said Ichiro.

"Right. And when you get home tell your mother to find the big saw and ask someone coming up to the mountains to bring it to me, okay? Now, don't forget. It takes me exactly an hour and a half, so even if you take your time I'm sure you can make it back home in three and a half hours. Even if you get thirsty, don't eat the snow."

"Okay," replied Narao. He had completely recovered his good spirits and was jumping around in the snow like a rabbit.

After the man had finished loading all the bags of charcoal and secured them to the horse's back with a piece of rope, he turned to the boys' father, "We'll be goin' now. Perhaps it'd be best to have the young'uns walk ahead."

"No, no, they're fine just following along behind. I'm much obliged to you now," the father smiled and nodded to the man.

"Well then, good-bye," the man took hold of the horse's tether and set out. The harness bells jingled as the horse walked at a slow place, its head lowered.

Ichiro had Narao go ahead of him and followed along behind. The snow on the path was packed down hard and pleasant to walk on. The sky was such a cloudless blue that there was something a little forbidding about it.

"Hey, there's something hanging in bunches in that tree," Narao suddenly shouted.

From his position at the rear Ichiro had not heard clearly. "What?" he asked.

"In that tree over there there's something hanging down in bunches," Narao explained again.

Ichiro looked and saw a lone tree standing at the base of a rocky ledge. From its branches brown fruit hung down in dense clusters. He stood gazing at the tree for a while. Then, realizing that the horse was

now a ways ahead of him, he hurried to catch up. Meanwhile, the man leading the horse had stopped and turned around to peer in their direction, but he had started walking again without saying anything.

The snow on the path was hard but it was bumpy in places and the horse frequently tripped and seemed about to stumble over. Narao was busy looking at all the things around him as he walked along and so he too frequently missed his step and came near to falling.

"Watch where you're putting your feet," Ichiro told him again and again.

The path had left the mountain stream behind and was now beginning to wind across a slope halfway up a large, elephant-shaped hill. There were several chestnut trees with lots of dry, rustling leaves still clinging to their branches. A bird with a slicing cry flew away behind them. Then the brightness of the sunlight grew somehow fainter, and the snow looked darker than before, but for all that, it started to shine more boldly.

A line of horses approached from up ahead, their harness bells jingling merrily.

The two parties met at a place where the path passed along side of a stand of spindle trees covered with red berries. Up ahead of the boys, the charcoal dealer's horse stepped off of the path and into the snow. The boys, too, gave way to the approaching group, stepping knee-deep into the snow beside the path.

"Good day."

"Good day to you," calling out a greeting, the men from the approaching party passed by with their horses.

The last man in the group, however, stopped as soon as he made his greeting. His horse walked ahead a little on its own but halted when the man uttered a "Whoa!" The two boys climbed back onto the path and the charcoal dealer's horse, which had been standing alongside them in the snow, also stepped back onto the path. Nevertheless, the two men started to converse about one thing and another.

The two boys stood for a while waiting for the charcoal dealer's horse to start walking again. But the wait got to be too long for them and after a while they began, little by little, to walk ahead. Ichiro thought to himself that once they had cleared the pass that lay in front of them they would practically be home. It was less than two and a half miles, and, although the weather had turned a little cloudy, the path was perfectly straight and so it was a simple matter to walk it on their own.

Out of the corner of his eye the charcoal dealer had seen that the boys had started walking on ahead, but he said nothing to them and continued his conversation, apparently planning to catch up with them shortly.

Narao appeared to want to get home as soon as possible, for he started to walk at a determined pace. Time and again Ichiro turned to look back, but all he saw were the horses in the snow, their brown heads drooping, and the two men in conversation, the white cloth covering the backs of their hands appearing and disappearing from view. He kept on walking.

The path began gradually to climb until at length it turned into a steep incline. Narao kept making a joke of it. He would plant his hands on his knees and make loud grunts of effort as he climbed.

Ichiro labored up the path following behind Narao, his breath coming in pants. He exclaimed excitedly at its steepness, calling it a true mountain trail.

At length Narao grew tired. He turned around and came to such an abrupt halt that Ichiro bumped into him.

"Are you tired?" asked Ichiro between panting breaths. When he looked back over the way they had come, there was only the narrow thread of the trail; both the man and the horse were below the line of the slope, blocked from view. Everywhere the white snow (this snow looked somehow dark and sullen, the sky was packed solid with white clouds and the sun, filmed over, shone like a huge silver platter) was gently rolling and here and there in the rises and hollows were scattered clumps of chestnut and oak, no more than three or four trees to a stand, and it was silent and inexpressibly lonely.

But Narao spotted a hawk swooping away down the slope from a spot above their heads and cried, "Shhh, there's a bird! Wooosh!"

Ichiro was silent, but after reflecting for a moment he said, "We should hurry up and cross the pass. It's going to start snowing."

No sooner had he spoken, however, than the top of the pass, with its smoothly undulating ridge line that had looked so dark against the shining white of the sky, grew hazy. A moment later a few tiny specks of powdery snow began to drift lightly down upon the two boys.

"Now, Narao, you've got to climb fast. It's started to snow. When we get to the top, the ground'll be level and it won't be so hard," Ichiro said in a worried tone.

Hearing the change in his older brother's voice, Narao immediately became alarmed and he began to scramble up the path.

"Don't rush too much. It's okay. We've got less than two and a half miles to go," Ichiro said between gasps of breath. But in fact the two boys couldn't help but hurry. They pushed themselves so hard they grew dizzy. It was too fast a pace for them to be able to keep up. The snow was falling thickly now, blotting out both the way they had come and the way they were going, and turning both boys completely white. Narao, who had started to cry, suddenly threw his arms around Ichiro.

"Do you want to turn back, Narao? Do you want to turn back?" Ichiro asked, not knowing what to do, but when he glanced down the slope in the direction they had come, it no longer seemed that they could turn back. That was because the way they had come was now solid gray and as murky as a pit. The direction of the pass, by comparison, looked white and brightly lit, and they were almost at the top. Once they got to the top the climb would be behind them. There would be a good mile of trail on the level. When they had come that way before, time and again pheasants had startled up into the sky and there had been bushes with red or yellow berries on them.

"There's just a little bit more now. Let's get going.

When we reach the top it'll stop snowing and the path will be level. Start walking, now. There's nothing to be scared of. Let's go. In a little while the man will come with the horse, so don't cry. We'll walk slowly this time."

As he spoke, Ichiro looked at Narao's face. Narao wiped away his tears and managed a smile. Ichiro watched as a snowflake landed on Narao's cheek and then melted away to nothing and he felt his chest tighten. This time Ichiro walked ahead. The path was no longer as steep as before. The snow, too, did not seem to be quite as deep, but even so, the boys' straw boots were soon buried.

As they drew near to the summit, black, jagged snow-topped rocks began to appear on both sides of the path.

The two climbed in silence one step at a time, trying as much as possible to stay calm. Ichiro wore a large piece of wool cloth around his shoulders as a cape and he flapped it in order to shake off the snow.

They were delighted to find they were at the top of the pass.

"We made it! We made it! The rest will all be on the flat, Narao." Ichiro turned to look behind him. Narao's face was bright red and he was breathing hard. He smiled in relief. But a fine, dense snow was falling, filling the space between the two boys.

"I bet the horse is half way up the slope now. Should I try calling?"

"Yeah!"

"Are you ready? One, two, three....HEL-LOO!"

His voice vanished into the sky in silence. There was neither a reply nor an echo, only the sky darkened with the snow that swirled steadily down.

"Well, let's get going. I'm sure we can make it down in half an hour."

Ichiro began walking again.

Suddenly, a howling gust of wind reached them from the sky. The snow billowed skyward looking like so much smoke or powder. They could not even draw a breath and the cold worked its way through the chinks in their clothes to chill their flesh. The two brothers stood with their hands pressed to their faces. After a while the wind subsided and they were about to set out walking again when a second gust, even stronger than the first, swept down upon them. It had a frightening sound like a ghostly flute. Their bodies were bent in two by its force and they were aware only of the snow at their feet flowing as smoothly as a river across their path.

The conditions at the top of the pass were very different from what earlier they had thought they would be. Narao felt so disheartened he started to cling to Ichiro, then he turned around and gazed behind him. But as soon as the wind died down a little, Ichiro started to walk again. The view behind Narao was so dark and forbidding that he pushed on, following unsteadily behind his older brother, crying noiselessly as he went.

The heels of their boots were clogged with snow. Here and there they encountered snowdrifts that made walking difficult indeed. Ichiro pushed on at a good pace all the same and Narao, too, put all his effort into following his older brother's footsteps. Ichiro kept turning around, but even so, Narao

tended to fall behind. When the wind made a loud whistle and the snow wafted up in a swirl of cold white smoke, Ichiro appeared to pause for a moment and Narao ran forward with tiny little steps and clung to his older brother.

Still, they were not yet even halfway across the top of the pass. The snowdrifts were enormous and time and again the boys stumbled.

Once, when Ichiro was crossing one of the drifts, the snow was deeper than he thought and he ended up getting his foot caught and falling. Ichiro's hands and body seemed to disappear into the snow. He made a squeaky sounding laugh as he got up, but Narao, who stood watching him from behind, sobbed with fright.

"It's okay, Narao. Don't cry," Ichiro said as he started to walk again. This time, however, it was Narao who tumbled over. He pushed his hands deep down into the snow, but he couldn't manage to get up right away, and he remained for a while crying with his head bent over as though he were bowing to someone. Ichiro ran back and lifted Narao up.

"It's just a little ways more. Can you walk?" Ichiro asked after he had brushed the snow from Narao's hands.

"Uh-huh," Narao nodded, but his eyes were filled with tears and he stared off into the distance, his mouth bent in a frown.

The snow fell steadily and the wind blew even more fiercely. They started to run again but they just kept stumbling in the snow. Ichiro tumbled over, and Narao tumbled over, and, to make matters worse, they were no longer sure they were on the path. A huge black boulder that they had never noticed before suddenly appeared to one side of where they were.

Another gust of wind bore down on them. The snow was like dust, like sand, like smoke. Narao panicked. He knew they were no longer on the path. The two had come face to face with the big outcropping of black rock.

Ichiro looked behind him. The trail of their footsteps made a furrow in the snow.

"We've lost the path. We've got to go back," said Ichiro as he clasped Narao's hand and started to run, but he took no more than a single stride before falling over into the snow.

Narao sobbed uncontrollably.

"Don't cry Narao. We'll stay here until the snow stops, so don't cry," said Ichiro as he stood at the base of the rock, hugging Narao tightly to him.

The wind rushed in a frenzy upon the two boys exactly as though it were a mad man. They stood, scarcely able to breathe, while the snow mounded steadily on their heads and shoulders.

"It's no good, it's no good," sobbed Narao. The wind carried away his words as though it were tearing them from his lips. Ichiro opened his wool cape and wrapped it around Narao so that it enveloped them both.

By that point, Ichiro had concluded that they would both surely die from the wind and the snow. All sorts of images circled before his eyes like a magic lantern show. Last New Year's they had been invited to the big house and they had gone and eaten mandarin oranges with the others. No sooner had Narao finished one mandarin orange than he had started in on the next, and Ichiro had given him a stern, scolding look. He could see Narao with his little red hands all chapped from the cold exactly as they looked that day. The sight made Ichiro feel as though he were taking a bitter poison and it hurt to draw a breath.

Ichiro realized that he was now sitting in the snow. He hugged Narao all the more tightly to him.

Three: The Dimly Lit Land

And yet everything seemed just like a dream. The cold, needle-like crystals of fine snow gradually lost their sting and turned warm. Narao, too, was no longer at Ichiro's side and Ichiro found himself all alone walking in a place that was like a dim, shadowy thicket.

The place was a hazy, yellowish color and he could not tell whether it was night or midday or evening. Some plant that looked like mugwort grew in abundance and here and there were black bushes that seemed to Ichiro to be breathing, exactly as though they were living things.

Ichiro looked down at his own body. Had he really been dressed this way before? His clothing consisted of nothing more than a single gray cloth wrapped around him. Startled, he glanced at this feet, which he now found to be bare. It seemed as though he had already come a long distance on those bare feet because they were deeply cut and dripping with blood. In addition, he felt very tired, especially in the chest and stomach, and it seemed to him as though his body were about to break in two. Suddenly, Ichiro felt very frightened and he broke into loud sobs.

"Where was he?" he wondered. But everything was deathly quiet and no answer came. Even the sky seemed utterly empty and the more he looked at it, the more he felt a strange, desolate fear. Then, abruptly, a new pain spread through Ichiro's feet and it felt as though they were being burnt.

All of a sudden, Ichiro thought of Narao.

He lifted his face to the dim, yellow sky and, still crying, shouted, "Naraooo!"

Everything was hushed. There was no reply at all. Ichiro could not endure the silence and he set out running, oblivious to the pain in his feet. As he started to run, the wind picked up and the cloth that wrapped his body streamed out behind him. When Ichiro thought of how he must look, crying as he ran barefoot with the tattered cloth trailing behind him in the wind, the fear and sadness that gripped his heart grew all the stronger and more unbearable.

"Naraooo!" Ichiro shouted again.

"Ichiro," ever so faintly, from far, far away came the reply.

Ichiro tore off in the direction of the voice. Still crying, he shouted time and again, "Naraooo, Naraooo!" Sometimes he thought he heard a faint reply and other times he was not sure.

Ichiro's feet were now entirely red. The blood had a lurid, bluish gleam to it and Ichiro could no longer tell whether his feet hurt or not.

Ichiro ran and ran.

Then, before him, he caught sight of a child who seemed to glow and fade, glow and fade, exactly like a candle flickering in the wind.

It was Narao crying with his hands pressed to his face.

Ichiro dashed to Narao's side, but his feet were unsteady and he fell. He scrambled up again and started to hug Narao. Narao continued to fade and then shine in rapid succession but, gradually, the pace of the flickering became so rapid that Ichiro could no longer detect the changes, and he held Narao firmly in his arms.

"Where can we be, Narao?" Ichiro said through his tears as he patted Narao's head. He felt as though he were dreaming and he couldn't tell whether the voice he heard was his own talking or someone else's voice that he was hearing in his dream.

"We've died," Narao said and burst out again into loud sobs.

Ichiro looked at Narao's feet. Just as he suspected, they were unshod and badly cut.

"There's no need to cry," said Ichiro as he gazed around him. In the far distance he could make out a hazy white light and that was all. It was hushed and he could hear nothing.

"Let's try going to that bright place over there. I'm sure there's a house there. Can you walk all right?" Ichiro asked.

"Uh-huh. I wonder if Mom will be there."

"Of course! I'm sure she'll be there. Let's go."

Ichiro led the way. The sky was a dim yellow color, without a hint of brightness, and it looked as though long arms might come reaching down from it at any moment.

Their feet hurt more than they could stand.

"Let's get to that place as soon as we can. If we can just get there, we'll be fine," urged Ichiro, trying to ignore the fact that his feet seemed to be burning with crackling white flames that caused him terrible agony. Narao, however, appeared unable to endure the pain any longer, and he fell to the ground crying.

"Hold on tight now, 'cause we're going to run there." Ichiro clenched his teeth against the pain as he hoisted Narao to his own shoulders. Then he set off running towards the hazy white light, all the while fighting back a hurt that was so intense it felt as though his body were being ripped to pieces. Even so, a number of times he fell, unable to endure the agony any longer. Each time he fell he pushed himself to get back on his feet once again.

When he glanced behind him, Ichiro saw that the way they had come was now hidden by a dim, gray veil of some mist-like substance. Behind the mist, he could make out something light red in color—he could not tell what—racing quickly away with a fluttering motion.

Ichiro was so frightened that he felt his breath catch in his throat. Nevertheless, he fought down the fear and forced himself to get to his feet and lift Narao to his shoulders. Narao's body was limp and he appeared to have fainted.

Crying, Ichiro spoke into his ear, "Narao, open your eyes, please! Narao, it's me, your brother!" He put all his strength into calling his brother back.

Barely, just barely, Narao seemed to open his eyes, but still only the whites were visible. All around them the ground seemed to be on fire, burning with white, flickering flames, so Ichiro used all his remaining strength to put Narao on his shoulders and start off towards their destination once more. He could no longer tell whether his legs were moving or not—it was as though his body were being ground beneath heavy boulders until it turned to a bluely gleaming powder and scattered into the air. Time and again he fell, only to lift up Narao again and, as though in a dream, start out once more running, holding Narao firmly in his arms. Eventually, Ichiro arrived at the brightish place he had set out to reach. It was, however, not a good place at all. Quite to the contrary. Ichiro stood transfixed, as though his body were frozen through, for before him was a depression in the ground that was like a valley and in the middle of it, from left to right, children in a truly pitiful state were being chased in droves. Some were clad in nothing more than a scrap of gray cloth, while others wore only a tiny cape against their otherwise bare skin. Thin, pale children whose eyes alone were large, small children with reddish hair, children with protruding bones who scampered with bent knees, all were running as though they were being chased, their bodies bent forward, full of fear, but with no time to even glance to the side, only sighing deeply, or crying without making a sound. All of the children had cuts on their feet just like Ichiro. And what was most frightening was that in amongst the children there strode creatures with bright red faces and the shape of large humans. They brandished thick whips and were clad in gray armor thickly grown with jagged thorns. Their hair was like a blazing fire, and their eyes were red and inflamed. The ground crunched loudly under their feet whenever they took a step. Ichiro was speechless with fright.

A child with curly hair and about the same size as Narao was in the line of children, but the pain in his feet seemed to be too much for him and he tripped unsteadily.

Just as the child was about to fall he blurted out with a sob, "Oh, Mommy, Mommy, it hurts!"

A frightening creature, who had been walking ahead of the child, stopped and turned around to face him. The child reeled and, raising his hands in fright, turned as though to flee, but, in that instant, the mouth of the frightening creature twitched and its whip cracked and, without a word, the child toppled over, writhing in pain. The children coming up from behind saw what had happened but simply hobbled aside to avoid the child. There was not one among them who uttered so much as a word. The child who had fallen over twisted in agony for a while on the ground, but before long he seemed to have forgotten the earlier pain in his feet, and rose unsteadily to stand.

Ichiro stood riveted to the spot, uncertain whether to advance or turn back. Suddenly, Narao opened his eyes.

"Daddy!" he shouted loudly as he burst into tears.

No sooner were the words out of his mouth, than one of the frightening creatures, who was just then passing below them, turned its crooked red eyes in their direction. Ichiro felt his breath catch in his throat. The frightening creature raised its whip and shouted up to them from below.

"Hey, what do you think you're doing up there? You come down here."

Ichiro felt as though he were being sucked into the creature's red eyes and took a few tottering steps forward, but presently stopped and stood his ground holding Narao securely in his arms. The frightening creature twitched its jowls, curled back its lips and then gave a loud roar as it climbed up towards Ichiro. Before they knew what was happening, Ichiro and Narao were snatched up and placed in the line of children. What saddened Ichiro most was the fact that Narao was somehow able to walk again and he hobbled along in front of Ichiro, his bare feet treading the cruelly painful ground. As he walked, driven along with the others, Ichiro softly called Narao's name over and over. Narao, however, seemed not to recognize Ichiro anymore. He simply put all his strength into walking on, often reeling from the pain or throwing back his hands in a gesture of fright. Then Ichiro reflected for the first time since arriving at the spot that the creatures chasing them were what were known as devils, and he wondered if Narao and all the children had done something bad that they were encountering such suffering here. Just then, Narao tripped over a red stone with sharp, pointed edges and fell. The devil's whip slashed down upon his small body looking as though it would cut it in two. Dizzy with fright, Ichiro clung to the devil's hand.

"Whip me instead. Narao hasn't done anything wrong."

The devil looked at Ichiro with a surprised expression. Then its mouth began to twitch and it spoke in a loud voice. Its teeth flashed with a glaring light.

"The sin is not one of this lifetime alone. Get moving."

Ichiro's back felt numb and everything before his eyes seemed to spin and turn blue. Then a cold sweat broke out all over his body.

In this fashion the two brothers were driven along. However, they seemed gradually to grow used to their situation, and they both felt it was getting a little easier. As though in a dream they observed off to one side the badly cut feet or fallen bodies of the others. Then, abruptly, their surroundings grew darker. Soon, everything turned black. Only the pale line of children being driven onward was visible within the blackness.

Once his eyes had grown accustomed to the dark, Ichiro could make out a wide field with many black creatures that were utterly still sitting in it. The scene had a faint, phosphorescent gleam. All of the creatures were completely covered with long, black hair, so that only the barest glimpse of their pure white feet and hands was visible. For whatever reason, one of the creatures seemed to move just the slightest bit, whereupon it uttered a piercing cry as though its body were being torn to pieces and began to run about in agony. But the shouting soon stopped and Ichiro saw it slump down so that it looked like a lump of mud. When his eyes grew even more accustomed to the lack of light, he realized that the creatures in the darkness were covered with hair that was as sharp as sword blades and that if they moved even slightly it cut their bodies.

After they spent a considerable time moving through the dark country, their surroundings grew a little brighter and they saw that the ground was now a crimson red. The children up ahead began to shout and sob wildly. The entire line of children came to a halt. The cracking of the whips and the devils' angry voices sounded like hail and thunder.

In front of Ichiro Narao wavered unsteadily. It seemed that the part of the field where they now were was made of something like broken bits of agate and all who went across it had their feet badly cut.

The devils had on iron shoes. When they walked it made a crunching noise as the agate was crushed beneath them. Now, on all sides of Ichiro the anguished cries went up. Narao, too, was in tears.

"Where are we going? Why are these terrible things happening to us?" Narao asked the girl next to him.

"I don't know. Oh, it hurts! Mommy, it hurts!" the girl sobbed as she shook her head back and forth.

"What are you talking about? All of you just brought this on yourselves. Why should there be any place you're headed?" growled one of the devils behind them as it snapped its whip yet again.

The grass in the field became coarser and sharper. Time and again they saw the children up ahead of them fall and then limply stagger to their feet. There were gashes on the children's feet and on their bodies and it got so that just the sound of a whip or a devil's shout was enough to make them start to topple over.

Narao suddenly seemed to remember who Ichiro was and he clung to his brother crying.

"Hey you, get going!" a devil shouted.

The whip lashed into Ichiro's arm as he held Narao. The arm went numb and he could feel nothing, only see the flesh throb. Since Narao still clung to Ichiro, the devil raised its whip once again.

"Please spare Narao. Please don't hurt him." Ichiro blurted out with a sob.

"Move!" The whip rang out again, so Ichiro used his two arms to shield Narao as best he could.

"Nyorai Juryō Bon Dai Jūroku (Book Sixteen on the Limitless Life Span of the Thus Come One)." As he struggled to shield Narao, from somewhere, ever so softly, as though it were a breath of wind or perhaps a scent, Ichiro sensed this phrase. Then somehow, it seemed that everything around him became a bit more bearable, and he tried repeating the phrase in a whisper. "Nyorai Juryō Bon (Book on the Limitless Life Span of the Thus Come One)." As he spoke, one of the devils who was moving up ahead stopped and looked around at Ichiro in amazement. The line of children stopped as well. Although it was not clear why, the cracking of the whips and the shouting voices ceased. A hush settled over the group. When they looked they saw that the edge of the dimly lit field of red agate had become a golden expanse and some being, looking very tall and splendid, was walking across it headed in their direction. For some reason, they all felt a sense of relief.

Four: The Shining Feet

The being's feet were white and shining. Very quickly, very directly he walked towards them. The pure white feet flashed in the light only twice before he arrived close to Ichiro.

Ichiro felt dazzled and could not lift his head. The being was barefoot. Those feet were large with a pearly shine exactly like that of seashells. The flesh around the ankles gleamed and hung to the ground. Indeed, they were huge, pure white bare feet. Yet those soft, unshod feet stepped upon the sharp, sharp chips of agate, and upon the red flames that licked upwards, without being cut or burnt in the slightest. Even the thorns on the ground did not snap beneath them.

"There is nothing to be afraid of," the being said to all the children with the softest of smiles. His large eyes gazed at them with the august magnificence of a blue lotus fully open. Without thinking, they all reverently pressed the palms of their hands together.

"There is nothing to fear. If we compare your sins to the power of the great virtue that envelops this world, it is like the difference between the tiny dewdrop that clings to the tip of a thistle thorn and the light of the sun. There is nothing at all to fear."

In a twinkling, the children had gathered in a ring around the being. The devils, who until then had seemed so frightening, now stood meekly behind them, their large hands folded and their heads bowed.

The being quietly turned his head to gaze at all the children.

"All of you have been badly cut. Those were wounds that you gave to yourselves. However, even those wounds are nothing at all."

The being patted Narao's head with his large, pure white hand. Both Narao and Ichiro could ever so quietly hear the hand give off a faint scent of flowers. Then the cuts on the bodies of all the children were healed and disappeared.

One of the devils burst into tears and knelt down in front of the being. It bent its head down to the cruel agate ground and humbly touched those shining feet with its hands.

The being once again smiled softly. Then a large ray of golden light formed a circle around his head and he spoke.

"Here the surface of the ground is made of swords that destroy your feet and bodies. That is what it seems to you, but in fact this ground is utterly smooth. Behold."

The being bent just a little and drew a circle on the ground with his pure white hand. Everyone rubbed their eyes and could not believe their ears. The distressing ground which up until then had been made of red agate thorns and had spewed forth dark tongues of flame, now changed into the perfectly smooth, waveless surface of a pure blue lake, the lake seemed to stretch on forever, ending finally in countless beautiful stripes the color of

malachite, and above the lake floated in utter stillness many splendid trees and buildings that looked like mirages, only they were more distinct. Those buildings were very far away but even so one had to lift ones eyes to take them in, some with roofs of blue and shimmering white, some trailing rainbow colored banners, some with aerial walkways spanning the empty air between them, the railings on the walkways gleaming like pearls, and a pagoda hung with bells and jeweled filigree, the tip of its slender pinnacle rising high into the sky. Peacefully, soundlessly, the buildings rose into the sky as their reflections fell in utter clarity upon the surface of the water.

There were also many trees. They seemed for all the world to be made of finely worked gemstone. There were deep blue trees in the shape of alders, and trees like willows that bore what looked like tiny platinum berries. On all the trees the leaves glittered brightly and made a delicate tinkling sound when one leaf brushed against the other.

Then sounds of various musical instruments began to drift lightly down from the sky together with many-colored lights that fell as fine powder. What was even more surprising was that the most magnificent looking people were thronging near and far. Some of the people were flying through the air like birds, but the silver-colored ribbons that bedecked their gowns extended in a straight line behind them without fluttering in the slightest. Everywhere the lovely scent of a summer dawn filled the air. Meanwhile, Ichiro suddenly noticed that his group, too, was standing on the utterly level, pure blue lake. But was it really a lake? No, it wasn't water they were standing on. Whatever it was felt hard. It felt cool. It felt smooth. It was in fact a sheet of some precious blue stone. Only it wasn't really a sheet; it was the ground itself. It was simply so smooth and shining that it looked like a lake.

Ichiro looked at the being who had spoken to them. His appearance was greatly changed from what it had been before. He stood behind them wearing the splendid hanging ornaments of a bodhisattva, his head crowned with a halo of golden light. He was more magnificent than any of the other people they could see there. Angels holding beautiful flower trays that seemed to be of interworked ruby and gold passed above the heads of Ichiro and the others, scattering large petals of cerulean blue and gold as they went.

Softly and quietly the petals drifted down from the sky.

All those who had been in the dimly lit field with Ichiro had now changed and become resplendent. Ichiro looked at Narao. Yes, he, too, wore golden robes, graced with splendid hanging ornaments. Ichiro then looked at himself. His feet now shone a pure white, the cuts and wounds completely healed. His hands gave off a dazzling fragrance.

For a while all the children simply raised their voices in joy, but presently one of them spoke.

"It's wonderful here. I wonder if that building over there is a museum."

The large, shining being smiled and replied, "It's not, although we do have museums. All the events in all of the many worlds are collected there."

Then the children suddenly began to ask all sorts of questions.

"Is there a library here?" one asked. "I'd like to read more Hans Christian Andersen stories and things like that."

Another said, "It'd be great if this were a playing field. If you threw a ball or something it would go forever."

"Oh, I want some chocolate," said a very small child.

The large being quietly replied, "We have many books here. There are some books that are lots of little books inside of one single volume. And then there are also tiny little books that contain all other books within them. I hope you will read a good deal. There are playing fields, too. Those who learn to run there can go even through fire unharmed. There is chocolate as well. The kind we have here is exceptionally good. I will give you some."

The large being glanced skyward. One of the angels flew straight down to him carrying a magnificent pot decorated with a pattern of yellow triangles. The angel alighted on the blue ground and then knelt respectfully before the large being and offered him the pot.

"Please try some," the great being said to all the children as he handed a piece to Narao. The next instant, each child was holding some of that wonderful confection. With just a single lick, the entire body felt cool and refreshed. When held on the tip of the tongue, it seemed to flicker, turning into blue firefly glow or flames the color of citrus or beautiful flower designs. After eating, one felt invigorated, and in a little while the entire body would emit an inexpressibly delightful fragrance.

"Where do you think Mom is?" Narao asked Ichiro as though he had suddenly remembered what had happened.

Hearing him, the large being turned in their direction, and, while gently stroking Narao's head, said, "In a moment I will let you see your mother from before. Soon you must enter school here. Also, you will need to say good-bye to your big brother for a little while, because he is going to return again to where your mother is."

The being said to Ichiro, "You are to return again to that earlier world. You are a good, gentle-hearted lad. It is a wonderful thing that you did not abandon your little brother in that field of thorns. Your feet that were ravaged then can now pass barefoot through the awful grove of swords. Never lose your present spirit. Many beings from this world have gone to your world and dwell there now. Seek them out carefully and from them learn the true way."

The being patted Ichiro's head. Ichiro could only stand with his eyes lowered and his palms pressed together. Then he heard in the sky a song sung with great energy by fine voices. The singing voices gradually changed and the entire scene grew hazy and distant as though veiled by mist. Beyond the mist a single tree stood shimmering white. Narao was truly shining and resplendent now and as he stood there he smiled softly as though he wished to say something and reached out his hand a little towards Ichiro.

Five: The Pass

"Narao!"

Ichiro thought he had called his brother's name when he suddenly saw something new that was pure white. It was snow. Then he saw blue sky, dazzling bright, stretching above his head.

"He's breathing! His eyes are open!"

The man with a red beard who lived next door to Ichiro was crouched down near Ichiro's head, trying his best to rouse him. Then Ichiro opened his eyes all the way. He was holding Narao tightly and buried in snow. The faces and red wool wraps and black overcoats of the villagers stood out clearly against the brilliant blue sky as they gazed down at Ichiro.

"What about the little boy? How's the little boy?" a hunter dressed in dog fur shouted loudly.

The man from next door took hold of Narao's arm to check. Ichiro watched too.

"It doesn't look good for the little boy. Build a fire as fast as you can," the neighbor man cried.

"No, it's a bad idea to build a fire. Lay him in the snow. Lay him in the snow," shouted the hunter.

As Ichiro was being helped to rise, he looked once more at Narao's face. It was as red as an apple and the lips wore the same soft smile as before when they had parted in the land of light. But his eyes were closed and his breathing had stopped and his hands and chest were as cold as ice.

Afterword

The author of this story, Kenji Miyazawa, was born in 1896 in the town of Hanamaki in the northern Japanese province of Iwate. The winters in Iwate are long and harsh. When Kenji was a boy, most of the people in the province made their living by farming or by laboring in the mountains, pasturing horses or making charcoal or cutting wood. In either case, whether working in the fields or in the mountains, life was very difficult. Many people were poor and whenever the weather was bad and the crops failed, there was sure to be famine.

Miyazawa's family lived in town and owned a pawn shop. While members of his family, too, worked hard for a living, they were considered prosperous; they did not need to worry about having enough to eat. As a boy, Miyazawa felt a deep concern for the poor farmers who came to the family shop, sometimes pawning their badly needed winter clothes or quilts in return for enough money to buy a little food. This deep concern was strengthened by Miyazawa's Buddhist faith, which constantly reminded him to feel compassion towards all suffering beings.

In a very real sense, Miyazawa devoted his own life to the goal of improving the lives of the rural poor in Iwate. As a young man, he studied agriculture. When he graduated from school, his father wanted him to take over the family shop, but Miyazawa was uncomfortable in that role and chose instead to teach local farm children in the new agricultural school that was founded in Hanamaki. While Miyazawa enjoyed teaching, he was not satisfied by a life in which he did not share the same hard work and suffering as the rural people. So, when he was thirty, he gave up teaching in order to farm and, at the same time, started an organization to help his fellow farmers. He worked hard at farming, but his body was not strong and in two years he had to give up his farming life after a serious bout of pneumonia. From that point on, he was frequently unwell. He died of tuberculosis at the age of thirty-seven at his parents' home in Hanamaki.

All the time that he was teaching, farming, working to start the farmers' organization, and even when he was suffering from illness,

Miyazawa was busy writing. He wrote both stories such as this one and also poems. In almost everything he wrote we can sense his love of nature, his understanding of science, his concern and compassion for others, and his strong Buddhist faith.

In "The Shining Feet" we meet three members of the rural community of Iwate: the boy, Ichiro, his younger brother, Narao, and their father. In Kenji's original Japanese story we can hear the two boys and their father speak in thick rural Iwate accents that tell us that they belong to a world before the homogenizing influences of television, mass media and jet travel. It is winter, and the boys' father is making charcoal in the mountains. We can assume that during the growing season he would farm fields near his village, perhaps grow rice. Charcoal-making gives him a means of earning a little additional income once the work in the fields is over for the year, but that occupation also condemns him to a lonely existence in the remote mountains away from his home village. We can imagine how pleased the father is to have his two sons visit him for the weekend.

For rural people like Ichiro, Narao and their father, the forces of nature—wind, rain, snow, etc.—were important matters, ever present in their thinking and experience. In his stories, Miyazawa frequently draws upon characters from folk tradition in order to invoke and personify these forces. One of the best-known of these characters is Matasaburo the Wind Boy. Miyazawa once devoted a whole story to the Wind Boy in which we learn that, like the wind itself, Matasaburo is elusive, tricky, difficult to pin down, at times helpful and at other times utterly destructive. In "The Shining Feet" we have a fleeting encounter with Matasaburo. Be sure to watch for him. And note, too, how honest Miyazawa is about the force and changing nature of the wind, and what that can mean to human beings.

Miyazawa's faith and experience as a Buddhist are very evident in "The Shining Feet." In fact, Miyazawa's Buddhist experience is probably more clearly and overtly expressed in this story than in any other story he wrote. In considering the Buddhist world that Miyazawa presents here, it is important to keep in mind the concept of karma, or cause and effect. According to the law of karma, performing good deeds results in good experiences and can lead ultimately to enlightenment. Bad deeds give rise to bad experiences and suffering. The consequences of good deeds and bad deeds, according to Buddhists, can last beyond one lifetime. In "The Shining Feet" Ichiro asks a devil why his brother Narao must suffer when he "hasn't done anything wrong." The devil invokes the law of karma when he gruffly explains that the bad deed, or sin, that occasions Narao's suffering "is not one of this lifetime alone."

The law of karma can seem stern and unforgiving when we consider it in a mechanical or quantitative way—X amount of evil deeds result in X amount of suffering, etc. There is, however, another, equally Buddhist way of looking at karma and suffering that allows us to see the psychological factors involved. By acting on our selfish desires, disregarding the needs of others, we feed these desires and reinforce a narrow and mistaken sense of self that makes us prone to suffering. By letting go of desire and attachment to self, we enter a state in which suffering no longer exists. In other words, suffering is, quite literally, all in the mind. By changing the way we think, we can turn a world of suffering into a world of joy. Good deeds and good thoughts can help us to make this change. This is what the smiling being in "The Shining Feet" means when he tells the children that the ground beneath their feet, which the children experience as made of cruelly sharp swords, is, in fact, utterly smooth and pleasant. The children's eventual escape from hell and arrival in heaven in "The Shining Feet" is not a physical journey, but a mental and spiritual one.

It is Ichiro who leads the children in this act of mental conversion, and in making this crossover from a world of suffering to a world of joy, Ichiro is inspired above all by certain curious words that he hears floating on the wind—*Nyorai Juryō Bon Dai Jūroku*. In English this means, Book Sixteen on the Limitless Life Span of the Thus Come One. Miyazawa was a Nichiren Buddhist, and unless we know something about this particular faith it is difficult to understand why this phrase should have such a profound influence on Ichiro and, eventually, all the other children.

For Nichiren Buddhists, the Lotus Sutra is a very sacred text that contains all the truth of Buddhist teaching. The words that Ichiro hears refer to Book Sixteen, or the Sixteenth Chapter, of the Lotus Sutra. This chapter describes the glorious and timeless nature of the Buddha who is called a *nyorai* (Thus Come One), one who has brought knowledge of the truth of reality to suffering beings. Miyazawa himself was not raised as a Nichiren Buddhist; he converted to that sect. His family belonged to a different sect of Buddhism called Pure Land. We know that when he was about seventeen Miyazawa read the Lotus Sutra for the first time and was deeply moved by it, especially, his friends say, by the Sixteenth Chapter. In the story of "The Shining Feet," Miyazawa conveys to his readers some of the sense of the transforming power that he himself experienced in reading the Lotus Sutra. Some of the scenes of heaven he creates in "The Shining Feet" echo the resplendent, visionary images of the Sixteenth Chapter. We usually think of stories as having either happy endings, in which all turns out well in the end for the characters about whom we care the most, or sad endings, in which the characters who matter most to us end up hurt or disappointed in some way. In "The Shining Feet," however, Miyazawa manages to give us a story whose ending is both happy and sad at the same time. It is not as though it were mixed in some way—mostly happy with a drop of sadness, or vice versa but both at once, both completely happy and completely sad. It is rather like one of those pictures with a grooved surface that changes depending upon how we hold it—turn it a little to the right and we see one scene, turn it to the left and we see another scene entirely. At the close of "The Shining Feet" we see two scenes and, indeed, two endings almost at once. Our minds flash back and forth between the cold, harsh but beautiful world of rural Iwate, and the glorious, visionary world inspired by the Sixteenth Chapter of the Lotus Sutra. Back and forth our eyes go, first to the one scene, then to the other. In moving back and forth in this way between a here-and-now world and a visionary one, between a world of suffering and a world released from suffering, between a sad ending and a happy one, we are beginning to think and experience things as Miyazawa Kenji did. Long after we have finished the tale, this flickering continues.

Sarah Strong
Lewiston, Maine
July 10, 1996

Translator: Sarah M. Strong

Sarah M. Strong was born in Key West, Florida in the United States in 1947. She received a B.A. in History from Oberlin College in Ohio in 1969 and a Ph.D. in Japanese Literature from the University of Chicago in 1984. Her Ph.D. thesis was on the poetry of Kenji Miyazawa. Since 1983, she has taught Japanese language and literature at Bates College in Lewiston, Maine, where she is currently an associate professor. Professor Strong has written on many topics in Japanese literature, including classical poetry and medieval Noh plays, but the works of Kenji Miyazawa remain her favorite topic of study. Her translation of Miyazawa's story "Night of the Milky Way Railway" (*Ginga Tetsudo no yoru*) was published in 1991.

Acknowledgements

I would like to thank Mr. Ichiro Takeda of International Foundation for the Promotion of Languages and Culture in Tokyo for his thoughtful advice and for his willingness to come all the way to distant Maine in snowy January to consult with me about this translation. I am also grateful to Mr. Keiichi Kajikawa and Mr. Toshio Takahashi of the same foundation for their support. I am grateful to Ms. Keiko Ueda of the Institute for International Education of Towa University for her friendship, advice and warm hospitality during my trip to Tokyo in June of 1996. I wish to thank Bates College for a summer research grant that made that visit to Tokyo possible. I am also grateful to Professor Shiro Hara of Waseda University whose leadership and whose monumental *Miyazawa Kenji goi jiten* have helped and inspired many of us involved with Kenji Miyazawa studies around the world.

Illustrator: Miyuki Hasekura

She was born in Hokkaido in Japan in 1963. She expresses her idea that the cosmos treats everybody equally through her poetry, pictures and other arts. She is a mother of three boys.

The Shining Feet ひかりの素足

英語版 宮沢賢治絵童話集 1

1997年1月30日　初版印刷
1997年2月10日　初版発行

協力	宮沢賢治記念館、宮沢賢治イーハトーブ館
原作	宮沢賢治
翻訳	©サラ・ストロング 1997
ブックデザイン	鈴木成一デザイン室
本文イラスト	©支倉美雪 1997
校正	アーネスト・マーヴィン・スミス
発行所	（財）国際言語文化振興財団 東京都新宿区高田馬場1-32-13 サンマークビル TEL: 03-5273-6660 FAX: 03-5273-6661
発行人	枻川恵一
発売元	（株）サンマーク 東京都新宿区高田馬場1-32-13 サンマークビル TEL: 03-5272-3166 FAX: 03-5272-3167
印刷所	大日本印刷株式会社
製本	（株）若林製本工場

ISBN4-7631-2311-4 C8390